Elizabeth Pannel is a secondary teacher living in Gilchrist, Oregon. She resides in this little town with her two puppies, Tanny and Chester. She enjoys writing, reading, singing, and teaching her fabulous students!

The Adventures of Larry McLou

Elizabeth Pannel

AUSTIN MACAULEY PUBLISHERS™
LONDON • CAMBRIDGE • NEW YORK • SHARJAH

Ordering Information
Quantity sales: Special discounts are available on quantity purchases by corporations, associations, and others. For details, contact the publisher at the address below.

Publisher's Cataloging-in-Publication data
Pannel, Elizabeth
The Adventures of Larry McLou

ISBN 9781647508074 (Paperback)
ISBN 9781647508081 (ePub e-book)

Library of Congress Control Number: 2021914570

www.austinmacauley.com/us

First Published (2021)
Austin Macauley Publishers LLC
40 Wall Street, 33rd Floor, Suite 3302
New York, NY 10005
USA

mail-usa@austinmacauley.com
+1 (646) 5125767

To Delores Irvin, for giving me the knowledge and courage to pursue my dreams (and this book).

To George and Nancy Pannel, for inspiring me to succeed and encouraging me to pursue all things creative.

I would like to thank Austin Macauley Publishers for helping make this book a reality and making a life-long dream come true.

High up in the sky,
where the birds fly on by,
floats Larry McLou,
who's not sure what to do.

Living over a town,
always wearing a frown.
He has to stand guard,
no matter how hard.

You see, clouds work too:
they have great work to do!
They give us shade from the sun
and water for rivers to run.

But one day old Larry,
who wasn't so merry,
had gotten the notion
to sail across the ocean.

"My life's such a bore!
I can't take it anymore!
I want to go somewhere new,"
exclaimed Larry McLou.

He abandoned his post,
traveling from coast to coast.
He saw many new places,
and greeted many new faces.

He stopped in Kalamazoo,
then to Lime, Peru.
He sunbathed in Belize,
he saw all seven seas!

He visited Cape Town,
and then Puget Sound.

He stopped in La Pine,
and thought it just fine!

But after a while,
he stopped wearing a smile.
He felt all alone,
so he headed back home.

He arrived with a fright!
What a terrible sight!
The crops were all dead,
he could see the riverbed.

So Larry lent a big hand,
bringing life back to the land.

After some time,
the wildlife was fine.

The town, it was saved!
After all it had braved!
And Larry McLou,
had learned something too.

It's great to vacation,
from nation to nation.
And it's okay to roam,
but there's no place like home.

CPSIA information can be obtained
at www.ICGtesting.com
Printed in the USA
BVHW061126011021
617801BV00011BA/420